Coyote's New Suit

Thomas King

Illustrated by Johnny Wales

KPk
Key Porter Kids

Library and Archives Canada Cataloguing in Publication

King, Thomas, 1943–
    Coyote's new suit / Thomas King ; illustrated by Johnny Wales.

ISBN 1-55263-497-3

I. Wales, Johnny II. Title.

PS8571.I5298C695 2004   jC813'.54   C2004-903931-8

The Canada Council | Le Conseil des Arts
for the Arts | du Canada

ONTARIO ARTS COUNCIL
CONSEIL DES ARTS DE L'ONTARIO

The publisher gratefully acknowledges the support of the Canada
Council for the Arts and the Ontario Arts Council for its publishing
program. We acknowledge the support of the Government of Ontario
through the Ontario Media Development Corporation's Ontario Book
Initiative.

We acknowledge the financial support of the Government of Canada
through the Book Publishing Industry Development Program (BPIDP)
for our publishing activities.

KPk is an imprint of
Key Porter Books Limited
70 The Esplanade
Toronto, Ontario
Canada M5E 1R2

www.keyporter.com

Text design: Peter Maher
Electronic formatting: Jack Steiner

Printed and bound in China

04 05 06 07 08 09 6 5 4 3 2 1

A long time ago when animals and human beings still talked to each other, Coyote had a wonderful suit that he wore everywhere he went.

Each morning Coyote would walk down to the pond. "Look at my fine suit," Coyote told everyone he saw, stopping only to hug himself and blow kisses at his reflection in the water. "Isn't it the finest suit you've ever seen? I must be the best-dressed creature in the entire world."

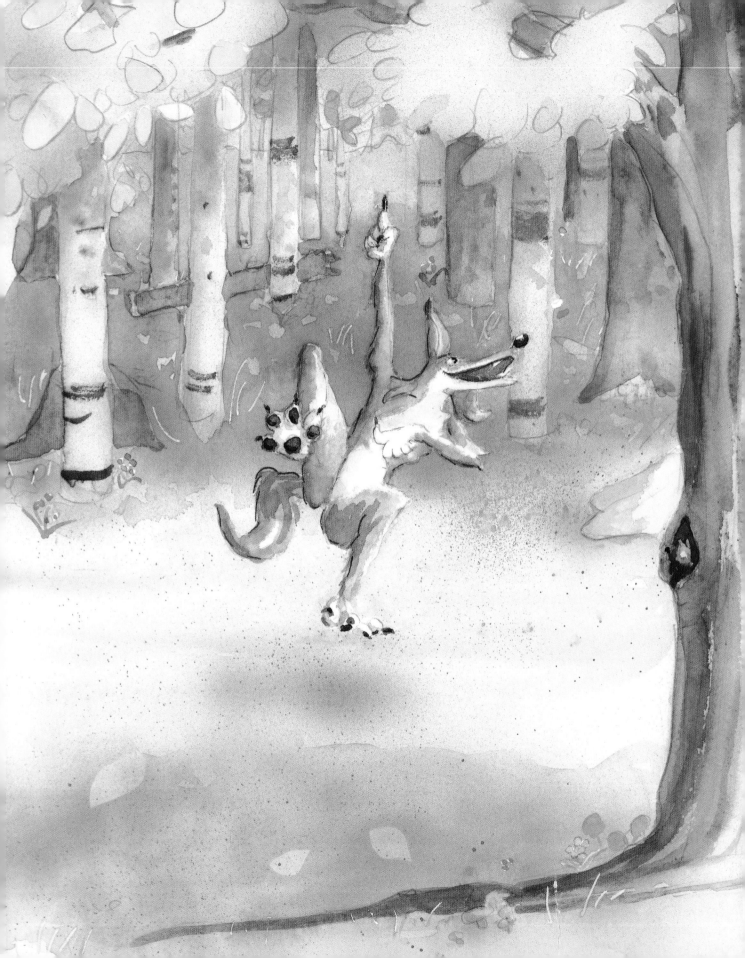

One day, when Coyote got to the pond, he found Raven sitting on a branch.

"Good morning," he said. "What are you doing here?"

"Oh, I thought I'd come by to see if anyone needed my help," said Raven.

"As a matter of fact," said Coyote, "you could be very helpful. What do you think of my suit? Isn't it the most excellent suit you've ever seen?"

Raven flapped her wings and stretched her neck. "It's okay, I guess," she said.

"Okay?" said Coyote. "It is certainly more than okay."

"Actually," said Raven, "it's pretty ordinary. And tan isn't a very exciting color."

"It's not ordinary," said Coyote, "and it's not tan! It's golden, toasty brown."

Raven fluffed her feathers and yawned.

"Feel how soft it is," Coyote continued. "Watch how it shimmers in the light when I dance." And Coyote danced a little, so Raven could see what a truly marvelous suit it was.

Just then Bear came out of the woods, all hot and sweaty. She took off her bear suit, folded it up neatly, and left it on a large, flat rock. "Wheeeeeee!" she shouted as she hopped into the pond. She waved her arms and kicked her legs and splashed water all over the place.

"Now that's a suit," said Raven, eyeing Bear's suit as it lay on the rock. "I don't believe I've seen a suit like that in my entire life." And she flew away.

But she didn't go far.

"Hummmph!" grumped Coyote. "What does Raven know about fashion?"

But he had to admit that Bear's suit did look substantial. When no one was looking, he tiptoed over and held the suit up to the light, rubbing his nose in the thick fur. "It's not as classy as my suit, but it certainly is impressive."

Then Coyote had an idea. It wasn't a good idea, but then most of Coyote's ideas weren't. "Perhaps," thought Coyote, "I should borrow this suit for a while. Then I can see whether classy or impressive suits me better."

So, while Bear was shampooing her hair and wiggling her toes and blowing bubbles in the water, Coyote piled her suit onto his shoulders and carried it home.

And no one saw him do this—no one except Raven.

When Bear came out of the water, her suit was gone. "What happened to my suit?" she asked, looking around. "It was right here a minute ago."

Raven hopped along the branch until she was next to Bear. "Hello," said Raven. "You're looking a little bare."

Bear was quite grumpy and in no mood for jokes. "Someone has stolen my suit," she said.

"Really," exclaimed Raven. "I can't imagine who would do such a thing."

"What am I going to do?" asked Bear. "I can't walk around the woods in my underwear."

"Perhaps I can help," said Raven. "Have you heard about the free clothes at the edge of the woods?"

"Free clothes?" said Bear.

"Oh, yes," said Raven. "Coyote told me about a camp of human beings at the edge of the woods who hang clothes they no longer need on ropes near their houses."

"Clothes they no longer need?" said Bear.

"And anyone who needs clothes can help themselves."

"I never knew human beings were so generous," said Bear.

"But don't let them see you," warned Raven. "Coyote says the human beings have strange ways. They are very shy, and they don't want to know who takes their clothes."

"That was certainly helpful," said Bear, and she hurried off through the woods to find the camp.

This could be a lot of fun, thought Raven.

When Bear reached the camp, she saw a rope tied between two trees. And hanging from the rope were all sorts of clothes.

"Oh, dear," said Bear, as she tried to squeeze into a floral tank top and a pair of gold-foil pedal-pushers. "How can human beings stand to wear such things?"

When Coyote got home, he tried on Bear's suit. It was a little too large and a little too heavy, and when Coyote tried to walk it made him trip.

"It's not exactly my size," he said, as he picked himself up off the floor. "But I certainly look stunning."

Coyote wore Bear's suit to the supermarket. He wore it to the baseball game. He wore it to bingo. And then he hung the suit in his closet and forgot about it.

"The only thing better than having one wonderful suit," said Coyote, "is having two."

The next day Coyote went down to the pond to lie on a rock and admire himself. When he got there, he saw Porcupine swimming laps. And there on a log, neatly folded up, was Porcupine's suit.

"Hmmmmm," said Coyote, touching the ends of the quills. "It's not classy and it's not impressive, but it is quite sporty—and everybody needs a sporty suit from time to time." And Coyote gathered up Porcupine's suit and scampered home.

When Porcupine finished swimming laps and came back to the log to do some stretching exercises, he noticed that his suit was missing. He looked on all the logs. He looked under all the rocks. But he couldn't find his suit anywhere.

"Hey!" shouted Porcupine. "Who took my suit?"

"Did you lose something?" asked Raven, who had seen everything.

"Someone took my suit," said Porcupine.

"Dear me," said Raven. "Who could have done such a thing?"

"This will never do," said Porcupine, pulling his underwear up around his chest as far as he could. "I can't walk around like this."

"Maybe I can help," said Raven. "Just the other day, Coyote told me something very interesting." And Raven told Porcupine about the camp at the edge of the woods and the human beings who liked to give away their clothes.

"Really?" said Porcupine.

"Just don't let them see you," said Raven. "They are a little strange and very shy, and they don't want to know who takes their clothes."

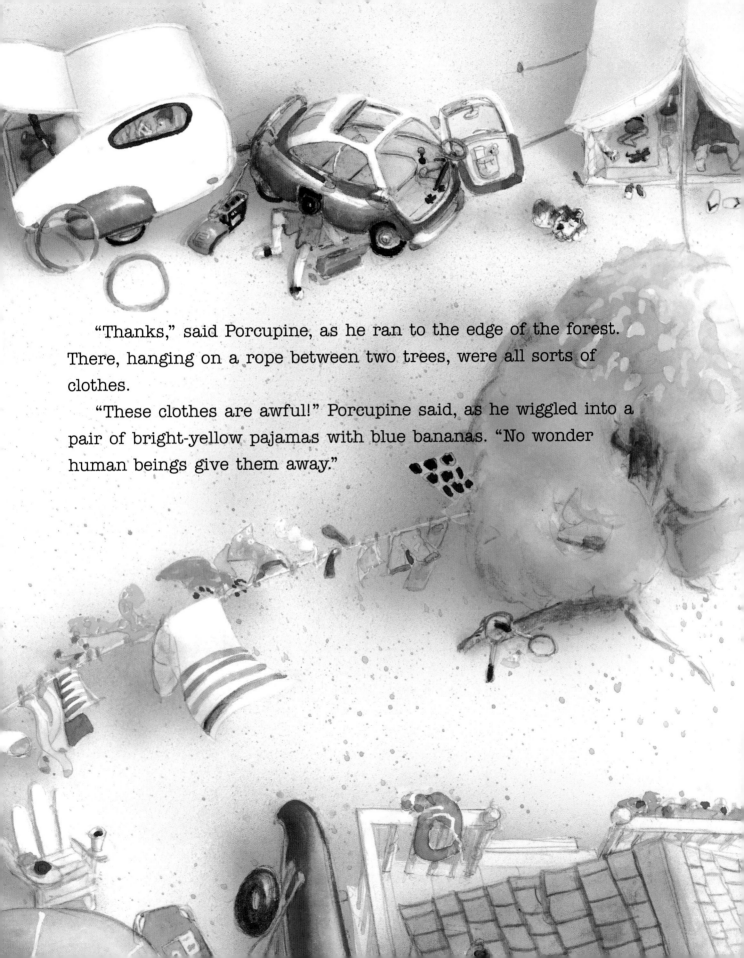

"Thanks," said Porcupine, as he ran to the edge of the forest. There, hanging on a rope between two trees, were all sorts of clothes.

"These clothes are awful!" Porcupine said, as he wiggled into a pair of bright-yellow pajamas with blue bananas. "No wonder human beings give them away."

Porcupine's suit was a little small for Coyote. He had to suck in his stomach and pull in his shoulders and hold his breath just to get it on.

"Lovely," he said, as he admired himself in the mirror. "Look at those quills. I can wear it to all the sporty places."

Coyote wore Porcupine's suit to the supermarket. He wore it to the baseball game. He wore it to bingo. And then he hung it in his closet and forgot about it.

"The only thing better than having two wonderful suits," said Coyote, "is having three."

The next day, Coyote got to the pond just in time to see Skunk and Raccoon and Beaver and Moose playing water polo. And folded up neatly on a large stump were their suits.

"Oh, happy day," cried Coyote, and while Skunk and Raccoon and Beaver and Moose were chasing the ball around the pond, he scooped up their suits and raced home.

When Skunk and Raccoon and Beaver and Moose finished their game and climbed out of the water, they were surprised to find that their suits were no longer on the stump.

"What happened to our suits?" asked Skunk.

"They were right here," said Raccoon.

Raven fluttered out of the tree. "Is there a problem?" she asked.

"Someone has stolen our clothes," Beaver explained.

"And all we have left is our underwear," said Moose.

"I think I might be able to help," said Raven. And she told Skunk and Raccoon and Beaver and Moose all about the human beings and the camp at the edge of the woods and the free clothes hanging on the line.

"Just don't let them see you," she warned.

Skunk and Raccoon and Beaver and Moose ran through the woods and crept to the edge of the camp. When no one was looking, they tippy-toed to the clothesline.

"Yaagggh," said Skunk. "I think I'd rather be naked."

"Me too," said Raccoon.

"Me too," said Beaver.

"Me too," said Moose.

In the meantime, Coyote was at home trying on his new suits.

"This one is perfect for formal occasions," he said, trying on Skunk's suit.

"The mask is terribly chic," he said, wiggling into Raccoon's suit.

"Leather is always in fashion," he said, adjusting the tail on Beaver's suit.

"Perfect," he said, wrapping Moose's large suit around himself several times. "Just the thing for lounging around after a hard day's work."

Coyote wore his new suits to the supermarket. He wore them to the baseball game. He wore them to bingo. Then he hung them in his closet and forgot about them.

One day, Coyote came home from the pond with Chipmunk's suit. "It doesn't really fit, but it certainly is lovely," said Coyote, forcing his arm into the sleeve. "And one can never have too many suits."

But when Coyote went to hang his new suit in the closet, he discovered that there was absolutely no more room.

"Oh, dear," he said. "Now what will I do?"

"Perhaps I can be of some help," said Raven, who just happened to be in a nearby tree.

"Why would you help me?" asked Coyote suspiciously.

"Because I'm your friend," said Raven, smiling as sweetly as she could.

"You are?" said Coyote, scratching his head.

"Certainly," said Raven. "Why don't you have a yard sale and sell all of your old suits."

"What an interesting idea," said Coyote. "Why didn't I think of that?"

"You get things ready," said Raven, "and I'll tell everyone about your marvelous sale."

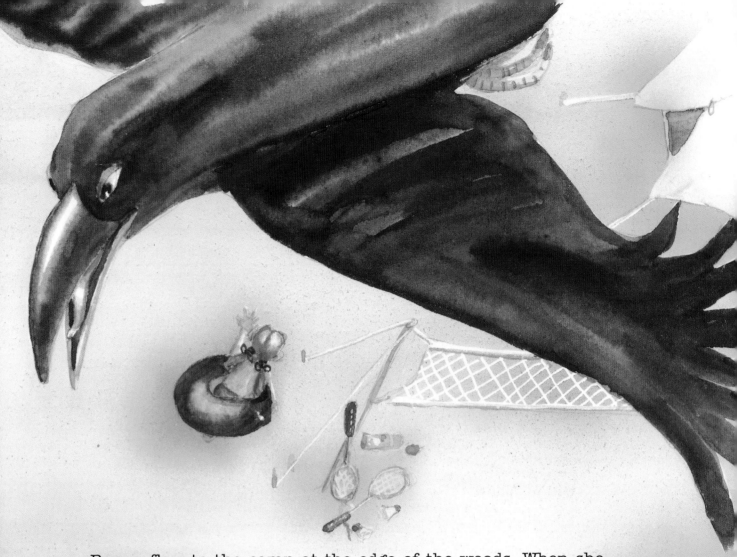

Raven flew to the camp at the edge of the woods. When she arrived, the human beings were all running around in their underwear.

"Goodness," said Raven, "is this what human beings wear?"

"Certainly not," said the human beings. "Every time we wash our clothes and hang them on the line, someone comes along and steals them."

"Are you in luck!" exclaimed Raven. "Coyote is having a yard sale and he just happens to have an excellent selection of clothing."

"Well, we certainly can't keep running around in our underwear," said the human beings. "Let's go see Coyote."

And while the human beings headed off to Coyote's yard sale, Raven flew back to the woods to find the animals. They were gathered by the pond in their human-being clothes, looking very grumpy.

"What do you want?" they growled.

"I just came by to tell you that Coyote is having a yard sale," said Raven. "And he has a great many fine suits to sell."

"Suits?" asked the animals.

"Oh, yes," said Raven. "I'm sure you'll find everything you need."

"Let's go," said the animals. "These human-being clothes are driving us crazy."

As the animals set off for the sale, Raven quickly flew back to Coyote's house.

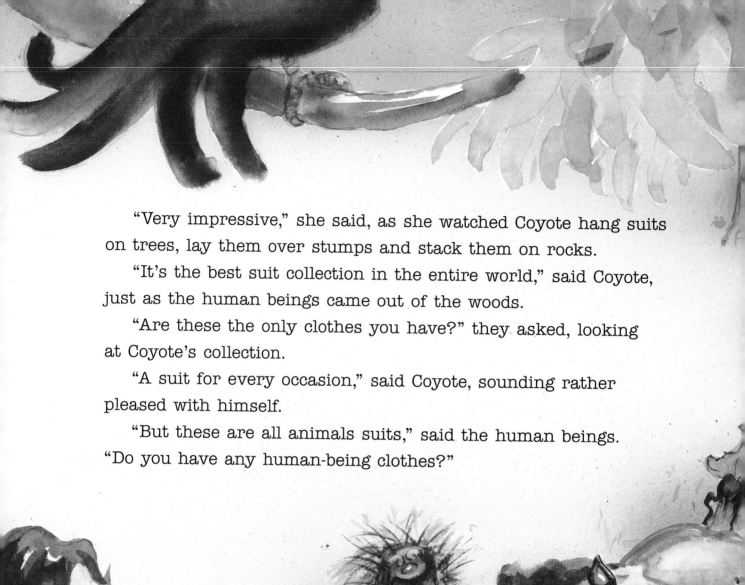

"Very impressive," she said, as she watched Coyote hang suits on trees, lay them over stumps and stack them on rocks.

"It's the best suit collection in the entire world," said Coyote, just as the human beings came out of the woods.

"Are these the only clothes you have?" they asked, looking at Coyote's collection.

"A suit for every occasion," said Coyote, sounding rather pleased with himself.

"But these are all animals suits," said the human beings. "Do you have any human-being clothes?"

"Oh, these suits are much nicer," said Coyote.

"But they smell funny," said the human beings.

Coyote wrinkled his nose—the human beings smelled pretty funny themselves.

"Try them on," he suggested. "I'm sure you'll find them warm and snugly."

So the human beings tried on the animal suits, and while they weren't as comfortable as human-being clothing, everyone had to admit that the suits were soft and luxurious.

But just as the human beings were getting used to their newsuits, the animals came into the clearing, dressed in their human-being clothes.

Oh boy, thought Raven. And she hopped around in circles on a branch. Here comes the fun!

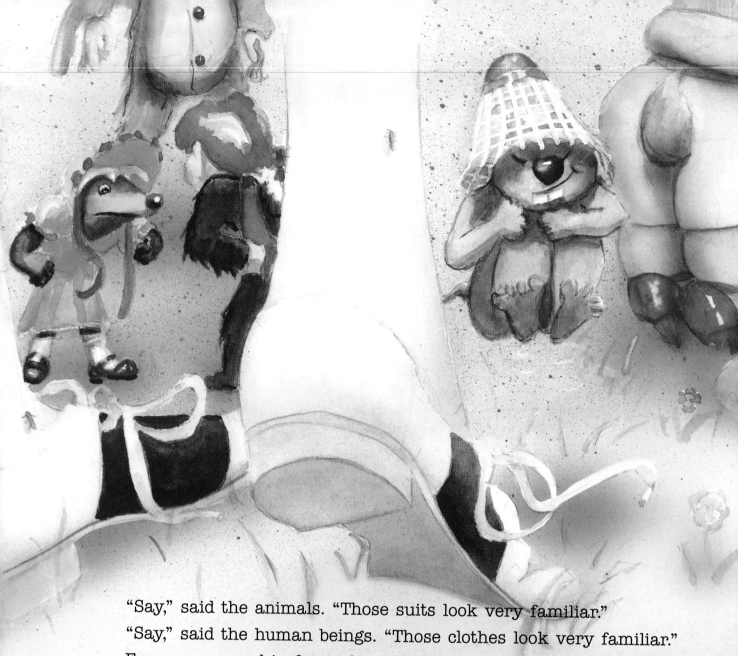

"Say," said the animals. "Those suits look very familiar."

"Say," said the human beings. "Those clothes look very familiar."

Everyone moved in for a closer look.

"Hey!" said Moose. "That's my suit!"

"Hey!" said a human being. "That's my dress!"

The animals and the human beings got closer and closer, until they were nose to nose.

"It was the human beings who took our suits!" shouted the animals.

"So it was the animals who took our clothes!" shouted the human beings.

And the human beings and the animals began to grumble and push and step on each other's toes.

"Stay calm," said Raven, as she flew down to a rock and fluffed her feathers. "I'm sure we can settle this in a civilized manner."

"Oh, yes," said Coyote, who was upset with all the grumbling and pushing and stepping on toes. "Let's all listen to Raven. She's very helpful."

"Okay," said the animals and the human beings, "but this better be good."

"First of all," said Raven, "we need to discover exactly who's to blame for this mess."

"Yes," said Coyote. "That's a good idea."

"The human beings are to blame," said the animals. "They took our suits, and they're wearing them right now."

"The animals are to blame," said the human beings. "We got these suits from Coyote. It was the animals who took our clothes, and they're wearing them right now."

"Coyote told us these clothes were free," said the animals.

"My, my," said Raven. "It sounds to me as though...Coyote is to blame."

"Coyote?" said the human beings.

"Coyote?" said the animals.

"Coyote?" said Coyote, who was trying to remember exactly where he had gotten his fine collection of animal suits.

"Of course, you could just trade clothes and suits," said Raven. "That way everyone will be happy."

"The sooner the better," said the animals.

"I don't know," said the human beings. "These animal suits are lovely and warm. And after a while, you get used to the smell."

"We want our suits back," said the animals.

"These suits would be very nice in the winter," said the human beings. "And we're not sure we want to give them back."

"Stop! Stop!" cried Coyote. "All this arguing is going to mess up the world."

"Mind your own business!" shouted the animals.

"Mind your own business!" shouted the human beings.

The animals and the human beings went back to grumbling and shoving and stepping on each other's toes until they were too tired to grumble or shove or step on each other's toes anymore.

"We didn't really want these anyway," said the human beings, and they threw the animals' suits on the ground. "They're much too hairy and smelly."

"Well, we certainly don't want these," said the animals, and they threw the human-being clothes on the ground. "They're much too tight and silly-looking."

And before Coyote could say anything, the animals and the human beings gathered up their suits and their clothes and stomped off.

"This is the last time we talk to you," shouted the human beings as they marched back to their camp.

"That's just fine with us," shouted the animals as they headed back to the woods.

After everyone had left, Coyote and Raven went down to the pond to relax.

"Thank goodness that's over," said Coyote. "All that arguing was giving me a headache."

"It was certainly exciting," said Raven. "I don't believe I've ever been to a more exciting yard sale."

"I don't know what all the fuss was about," said Coyote. "None of those suits is as wonderful as mine."

"It's okay, I guess," said Raven, "but tan is not a very exciting color."

"It's not tan," said Coyote, looking fondly at his reflection. "It's golden, toasty brown."

Just then Bear came out of the woods, took off her suit, and jumped into the water.

"Now that's a suit," said Raven. "I don't believe I've ever seen a suit like that in my entire life."

"You think so?" asked Coyote. He tiptoed over to Bear's suit and held it up to the light.

"Absolutely," said Raven.

"It's not as classy as my suit," said Coyote as he rubbed his nose in the thick fur. "But it is certainly impressive."

"Let me know when you have your next yard sale," said Raven, and she flew away.

But she didn't go far.

In case someone needed her help.